HADDOCK 'N' CHIPS

Haddock is a little, green, chip-crazy alien who visits the planet Earth – and once you've seen life through her eyes, you'll never view the world in quite the same light again!

Linda Hoy was a teacher for almost ten years before becoming a full-time writer. She is the author of a number of books for young people, including *Nightmare Park*; *Your Friend, Rebecca* and *Kiss*. She has also written an award-winning television play, *Emily*. She lives in Sheffield with an ancient cat called Scruffbag and enjoys heavy rock music, walking on the moors and scoffing vanilla slices.

Caroline Holden has illustrated many children's books, including *The Secret Diary of Adrian Mole aged 13¾*, *Clever Cakes*, *Roseanne and the Magic Mirror* and *The Human Zoo*.

Some other titles

Broops! Down the Chimney
by Nicholas Fisk

Change the King!
by Hugh Scott

Geoffrey Strangeways
by Jill Murphy

Jake's Magic
by Alan Durant

Second-time Charley
by Kathy Henderson

Stone Croc
by Penelope Farmer

The Summertime Santa
by Hugh Scott

Titch Johnson
by Mark Haddon

HADDOCK 'N' CHIPS

LINDA HOY

Illustrations by

CAROLINE HOLDEN

WALKER BOOKS
LONDON

To Lauren

First published 1993 by Walker Books Ltd
87 Vauxhall Walk, London SE11 5HJ

This edition published 1994

This book has been typeset in Sabon.

Printed by Clays Ltd, St Ives plc

British Library Cataloguing in Publication Data
A catalogue record for this book
is available from the British Library.

ISBN 0-7445-3174-8

Contents

Chapter One

"Are you Haddock 'n' Chips?"

The waitress wore a big smile on her face as she wafted a plate of sizzling food under my nose. There was something large and flat and golden, some round, green, mushy-looking vegetables and a pile of thin brown sticks. The food looked very strange to me, but it certainly smelled delicious.

My mouth was beginning to water.

I shook my head. "No," I told her. "I'm not Haddock 'n' Chips."

"Oh." She looked disappointed as she moved away. Then she went round the other tables in the café. "Haddock 'n' Chips?" she asked everyone.

"Here you are. That's me," said a fat man with a newspaper.

The woman smiled, then presented him with the whole plateful of food. "There you are, then. That's for you."

I saw the man lick his lips as he picked up his knife and fork.

It was then that I decided to change my

name to Haddock. It was a name I liked the sound of. I looked up the word in my *Intergalactic Encyclopedia*:

> **haddock** a fish found in the cold, northern seas of planet Earth.

Of course, I did have a name already – a Triangulum name. But if I told you my name you wouldn't be able to say it. First you would have to curl your lips into a sort of beak, then blow through them, making a very low grunt. Then you would have to push your tongue up inside your nose and wiggle it about, making a kind of whooowhoooo sound. As I say, no one on Earth can do that and they wouldn't really want to try.

So, that's why I thought it would be a good idea to change my name to Haddock.

I had been expecting a welcoming party when I arrived on Earth, but no one had been there to greet me. My teacher had sent my picture and the time of my arrival through ISES (the Intergalactic School Exchange System), but there was no one waiting when I climbed out of my spaceship. Only an empty field.

"Greetings," I said to the black and white creatures eating the grass, but they just kept their heads down and ignored me.

Never mind, I thought. I had some Earthpennies and a map of the area and my *Intergalactic Encyclopedia*. I just didn't have anywhere to stay.

"I'm looking for a house," I told the policeman I saw, later, standing in the street.

In my *Intergalactic Encyclopedia* it said:

> **policeman** he is there to help you. You can ask him the way if you are lost.

I was lost. I didn't know where I was going and I wanted to find a house. Everyone else seemed to live in one.

The policeman was talking to a box with a long pencil sticking out of it. He pushed the pencil back into its box and scowled at me. "A house?" he repeated. "Which one?"

Of course, I wasn't looking for any particular house. Any house would do.

I thought an empty one would be best but I wasn't very choosy. While I tried to think what to say, the policeman stared – rather rudely, I thought – at the three triangular antennae peeping from my space helmet.

"Where are you from?" he asked me.

"Triangulum."

He looked a bit confused, so I explained to him. "It's a triangular constellation a few light years away from Andromeda."

"Hmmm." The policeman stroked his moustache. "And what's your name?"

I smiled at him. "Haddock."

There was an uncomfortable pause.

"And what's your second name?" he asked.

"'n' Chips."

The policeman didn't offer me anything nice to eat. In fact he didn't do anything nice at all. Perhaps he wasn't one of the nice policemen in my book. He shouted very loudly into his box. I had a feeling he was getting cross.

I thought it best to jump inside my Earthmobile and whizz away.

* * *

It was early in the morning when I found the house that I was looking for. The house wasn't too big and it wasn't too small. It seemed just about right. It was surrounded by a garden filled with red and purple flowers. There were flowers growing up the sides of the house as well, forming a pink and white archway round the front door. The house had lots of windows, all with pretty lace curtains. There was only one problem – somebody lived in the house already.

I parked my Earthmobile in the middle of the road where there was an illuminated flashing sign of a red man – presumably, to show that this was a suitable place to leave your car and walk. Then I went back to see the house. As I arrived, the front door opened and some people came out.

There was a tall, thin man, a middle-sized woman and a small boy. But the person that made me take notice was the girl. She looked about my age – about two hundred and fifty turns of the Triangle, that is – and as soon as I saw her I realized that what I was already beginning to miss on planet Earth was having a friend to play with.

I watched the girl carefully as she walked out of her house. She was carrying a cat. I recognized it straight away because we have lots of cats on Triangulum although, like most other things on our planet, of course, our cats have only three legs. The girl placed the cat carefully on the doorstep and then she locked the front door. I saw her hide the key inside one of the flowerpots hanging beside the door. Then she climbed into a big brown vehicle with the man and the woman and the little boy. I stood in the bushes beside the gate and gave a little wave as they drove past. The girl was looking out of the window. I don't know whether she noticed me or not.

"Are you the owner of this vehicle?" the policewoman asked me.

I wasn't sure what to say. My Environmental Studies teacher had borrowed the Earthmobile for me. It actually belonged to DIE (the Department for Interplanetary Excursions). It wasn't really mine.

I said nothing.

"Have you parked it on a pelican?"

I quickly looked up "pelican" in my encyclopedia. There was a picture of a large white bird with spindly legs and a large orange beak. I certainly hadn't seen one of those. And I would never have dreamed of parking my Earthmobile on one. I shook my head.

"Can I have your name?"

I hesitated.

"You do have a name?"

I was becoming less sure, now, of my new name. "Haddock 'n' Chips," I mumbled.

"I beg your pardon?"

I began to back away along the street. "Haddock 'n' Chips," I shouted as I quickly checked for stray pelicans underneath my wheels. Then I leapt inside my Earthmobile and sped away.

DEPARTMENT OF INTERPLANETARY STUDIES

TOPIC SHEET 1: THE EARTH

1. What Are the Main Differences Between Planet Earth and Triangulum?
The main difference is that, on Earth, they have only recently discovered the Triangle, so most things are square or circular. The people still live in old-fashioned, square houses, although some have triangular roofs. They drive square Earthmobiles with little, fat, circular wheels. They do not travel very fast.

2. What Wild Creatures Live on Planet Earth?
There are some black and white, homeless creatures who live outside in

fields. They walk on four legs and have two rounded, white antennae. They are unfriendly and speak a strange language with a limited vocabulary, but they do not seem to be dangerous.

Chapter Two

I slept that night in my Earthmobile. I woke up with stiff arms and legs because there wasn't much room to stretch out and my tummy was a bit sore where it had pressed against the steering triangle. I had a good stretch when I got up and decided to go and visit Rosie's house again. I didn't know then, of course, that her name was Rosie. I didn't find that out till later. When I reached the house, I waited behind the hedge and watched as the family dashed outside.

That morning it was raining. I knew about rain because we'd already done "The Climate of Earth" in Interplanetary Studies. We'd learned that people on Earth drank rainwater, but I assumed they drank it because it tasted nice, like fruit juice or frothy milk shake. Because we'd learned about showers of rain I thought it would be hot as well, like the shower I get washed in at home. Rain was one of several disappointments about my trip to planet Earth.

The family were late this morning and the

tall, thin man was impatient. He climbed into his car, revving up the engine while Rosie locked the door and hid her key. She didn't bring the cat.

I watched them speeding down the driveway and I smiled and waved again, but the car was going too fast. No one seemed to notice.

I was just walking back to my Earthmobile (parked sensibly on a black-and-white-striped empty parking strip today) when I heard the sound of an animal. *Yeeooow*, it went. *Yeeooow*. It sounded like an animal in pain.

I stopped. I didn't really want to go back to the house because the rain was getting heavy. I was wet enough already. But then I heard the noise again. *Yeeooow*.

I thought I'd better have a look.

The yeeooowing came from the back of the house. I ran down the drive, round the corner, and found a back door with a square, metal flap cut out of the bottom. The flap was slightly open and I could see a furry, ginger paw peeping out. *Yeeooow*, the cat was squealing, with its paw stuck inside the letter box. Stupid animal, I thought. And what a silly place to put a letter box.

I tried to lift the metal flap to free the cat, but when I moved it the edge cut tighter into the furry paw. *Yeeooow,* it cried again.

"Go back inside," I told the cat. Then I lifted the little paw and tried to push it back inside the flap. *Yeeooow!* I yelled. The cat had scratched me with its tiny, sharp claws.

I sucked my fingers as I sat down on the back doorstep. I needed a plan of action. The best thing, I decided, would be to pull the cat backwards from inside the house. Then I remembered Rosie hiding her key inside the flowerpot. If I let myself into the house, I thought, then I could rescue the cat.

"I'll be with you in a twirl of the Triangle," I shouted through the metal flap. "Don't go away, now."

I walked round to the front of the house, the cold, wet rain that wasn't even nice to drink dripping from my hair and green blood dripping from my fingers. I stood on tiptoe and reached up to the flowerpot, then I took out the key, opened the door and went inside.

The house was beautifully furnished and very clean, without a speck of dust. There were arrangements of flowers on the highly-polished tables and there were colourful, woven carpets on the highly-polished floors. I tiptoed silently through the hall although I felt certain there was no one there to hear me.

Even the kitchen looked clean and tidy. Our kitchen tables at home are normally scattered in the mornings with little triangles of sticky toast coated with banana jam or with left-over cereal and half-drunk glasses of extra frothy milk shake. Here, there was neither cereal nor toast and nothing left to drink. There weren't even any children's toys or paintings for me to look at. There was a cat, though, lying on the floor, whimpering, with its paw stuck fast inside the door.

"Come on then, let's have a look," I said,

bending down and stroking the cat.

She snarled at me.

I took a deep sigh. Cats are just the same, right across the galaxy. She obviously didn't understand that I was only there to help her.

"Come on. It won't hurt," I said, starting to ease back her paw. It obviously did hurt her, when I lifted up the metal flap and prised her leg backwards. *Yeeooow*, she squealed again. But this time she was free.

Of course, she didn't try to thank me. Cats are never grateful. In fact after limping round the kitchen, she walked straight back to the metal flap as if she were about to stick her paw inside it once again.

And then my Triangle tingled. It wasn't a letter box at all. It was a special flap. A cat flap. And all the cat wanted was to go outside.

I unbolted the door and opened it and she wandered outside into the wet garden.

After I'd closed the kitchen door, I looked down at my hand. It had stopped bleeding now, but I knew I ought to wash it. The little green scabs of dried blood would already be covered in germs. I decided to go upstairs and try to find the bathroom.

I climbed the wide, velvet-carpeted staircase with its carved wooden bannister, but I never reached the bathroom. At the top of the stairs was a bright yellow door with a notice printed on it in red and blue crayon:

Rosie's Room

I opened the door and peeped inside.

When I saw the inside of Rosie's room I just stood still and stared. It was the nicest room I had ever seen in all my life.

Rosie's bed was surrounded by soft, white, lacy curtains, held up by shiny bedposts. There was a plump, cushiony duvet, just like mine at home, except that hers was covered in coloured patchwork cats. Sitting on it was a big fluffy white cat. Not a real cat this time. It had a zip along its tummy and something was half stuffed inside.

But that was not the only cat in Rosie's room. Not by a long, long way. There were different kinds of cats and kittens all along the wall. There were pictures of cats and shelves full of cats. There were glass cats and wooden cats and black cats and ginger cats. There were stone cats and stuffed cats and embroidered cats and tiny, weeny kittens. The table lamp beside her bed was shaped like a long, thin Siamese and the big cushion on the floor had a long, furry, ginger tail. Peeping from underneath the bed was a pair of white, furry slippers, but even they had pointed ears, long black whiskers and narrow, gleaming eyes.

I could have just stood there staring all day, but I didn't, of course. Over by the window was a desk, a chest of drawers and a wash basin. I walked across to bathe my hand.

I found some antiseptic lotion in the

cupboard above the sink and I put some in the water. Then I looked for something nice to rub on my hands afterwards to take the smell away.

Inside Rosie's cupboard were different-shaped bottles. I examined all the labels. A small round bottle held *Essence of Violet Hand Cream* and a large square bottle contained *Essence of Rosemary Shower Gel.* There was *Oil of Peppermint Shampoo and Conditioner* and *Oil of Peppermint Foam Bath.*

I took off the tops so I could smell them and try them out. I thought they smelled delicious, especially the *Oil of Peppermint.* That smelled almost nice enough to drink. I soon stopped trying out the bottles though, when I came to one labelled *Toilet Water.* I stared at the label in horror. Why would Rosie want to keep water from the toilet in such a nice bottle? I didn't know what to think.

Next to the sink was a tiny fridge. I peeped inside and saw bottles of orange juice and cartons of milk shake. There was strawberry flavour and banana, pineapple, and peach. Banana was my favourite and I noticed Rosie had two of those. I closed the door again quickly and tried to forget I'd seen them.

Before I went back to my Earthmobile, I just had to try out Rosie's bed. I slid off my spaceboots and lay my head down on the pillow for a minute, wrapping the cat duvet round my damp clothes.

The bed was very, very warm and cosy and the mattress was supersoft and springy.

And soon I fell fast asleep.

When I woke up, I felt strange. I couldn't think where I was at first. Then I remembered and I knew I must hurry away before anyone came home and found me.

I pulled on my silver spaceboots, then tiptoed on to the landing. Everything was quiet. I ran downstairs, picked up the door key from the kitchen, then dashed outside, locking the front door behind me and replacing the key inside the flowerpot. I was pleased it had stopped raining now. I ran down the driveway and back towards the busy street.

"Is that your vehicle?" the policeman asked me. He was holding a notebook in one hand and a pencil in the other.

I didn't know what to say.

"Have you parked on a zebra?"

I looked up zebra in my *Intergalactic Encyclopedia*. There was a picture of an animal rather like a horse. I began to shake my head.

"That vehicle's parked right in the middle of a zebra crossing."

The zebra in my book was covered in black and white stripes. I definitely hadn't seen one of those crossing the street.

"I've been looking for the owner all day."

I knew there were black and white stripes on the road, but surely it wasn't a squashed animal? I'd have noticed if I'd run over anything.

The policeman seemed to be staring – rather rudely, I thought – at my triangular nose and my pale green skin. On our planet we consider it impolite to stare at anyone who looks a little bit different.

"Well, I must tell you that anything you say may be taken down..." He scowled at me, licking his pencil.

I glanced up the street at my Earthmobile, parked quite tidily I thought.

"And used in evidence. Can I have your name, please?"

I decided to make a run for it. "Haddock 'n' Chips," I shouted, sprinting off down the street. "And it wasn't me that squashed the zebra. It was already flattened when I got there."

I checked under my triangular jets for any more stray animals. When I felt sure that all was clear, I leapt inside my Earthmobile, pressed the starter motor, twizzled my steering triangle and tore away.

DEPARTMENT OF INTERPLANETARY STUDIES

TOPIC SHEET 2: THE EARTH

1. What Do You Find Most Interesting About the Earth Dwellings?
All the cats. They have lots of toy cats and cat cushions and cat duvets and things.

Also, their beds are nice and comfy.

2. What Domestic Creatures Live on Planet Earth?
There are four-legged cats. They live in the rectangular houses with the people.

There are wild pelicans flapping along the busy streets. You have to be very careful not to park your Earthmobile on one. It is part of the policeperson's job to look after the pelicans so I think they must be an endangered species.

There are also zebras, who find it very difficult to cross the streets. Sometimes they get squashed and make stripy marks all across the road.

DEPARTMENT OF INTERPLANETARY STUDIES

TOPIC SHEET 3: THE EARTH

1. What do Earth People Drink?
Rain. I don't know why because it doesn't taste very nice. They do know how to make banana and strawberry milk shake, but then they hide their milk shakes away in little boxes inside their fridges.

2. What Do You Find Most Interesting About Earth People?
They do some things backwards. In my encyclopedia, for instance, it says that they splash toilet water on their faces after they have had a bath!

If I got toilet water on my face, I would want a wash straight afterwards!

Chapter Three

I thought about Rosie's room all night. I thought about it when it rained again and I got soaking wet. I thought about her cosy bed when the wind howled round my Earthmobile and made me shiver. And I thought about the cartons of milk shake inside her special fridge when I had to collect rainwater inside my space helmet so that I could have a drink.

I did have money to buy food, but the shops weren't open all the time. They closed when it got dark. I don't know why. Perhaps Earth people only eat in daylight. In deepest Triangulum we like to eat all the time.

The next day, I decided to go back to Rosie's house. I was managing all right on Earth. I'd already started work on the special assignment for my homework and I felt sure it would be finished before the spaceship arrived to take me back. The only real problem I had was loneliness.

I was used to having plenty of friends at

home. We used to visit each other in the evenings and play lots of games. We used to sit down and have long chats and share our banana milk shakes together by the fireside. But here on Earth, the only people who'd shown any interest in me were the police. None of them were like the nice policeman in my book and I didn't think any of them would make nice friends.

But I thought Rosie would make a very good friend. I felt as though we had a lot in common. I could just imagine myself, sitting on the furry cat cushion on her floor, sipping banana milk shake and telling her all about my planet and my school. I could just imagine her, telling me about her friends and bringing out all her games for us to play. I even thought I could live secretly inside her room – it was big enough for both of us – and then I could sleep in the afternoons inside her comfy bed while she was out at school. When I went back home again, we could become intergalactic pen pals. I might even persuade my teacher to organize a visit to our planet for her with the Intergalactic School Exchange.

The next morning when I arrived at Rosie's house, the family had already left. I thought it might be better if the grown-ups didn't see me. I strolled along the driveway, helped myself to the key from the flowerpot, then I unlocked the door and went inside.

This time I went straight upstairs to Rosie's room. I opened the yellow door and looked inside. I noticed a pile of books left out on her desk. They weren't there the day before. I walked across and had a look.

The book on top was Maths and it was open at the homework Rosie had been doing. What a mess! It was a page filled with crossings-out and rubbings-out and higgledy-piggledy numbers sliding all over the place. I scanned some of Rosie's calculations – they were only long multiplication to four decimal places, but even then she'd hardly got any right. She kept forgetting to carry ones,

I noticed. And twos. And threes. I sighed. I decided to sit down at the desk and help her out.

It took me nearly half an hour to sort out Rosie's homework. If I'd been doing it myself, from scratch, I'd have finished it in less than five minutes, but I had to spend a long time working out where Rosie had gone wrong.

I sharpened a pencil with Rosie's cat sharpener and wrote in, very faintly, all the correct answers for her. Then I drew little circles round her mistakes so she could understand where she'd been going wrong. Then I had a banana milk shake. I knew I shouldn't really, because they weren't mine to drink, but I did think I deserved one after all the hard work I'd done.

After I'd finished my milk shake, I began to inspect Rosie's cats. I took off my boots, climbed on the bed and took the cats down from the shelves one at a time. I enjoyed touching the cats, feeling and stroking each one in my hand, and I played a little game, holding them with my eyes closed and trying to guess what each cat was made of. I guessed the cold, glass cats and the squat, stone cats and the stuffed, velvet, tabby kittens. But I had difficulty with the black coal cat and the polished wooden ginger cat and some of the pottery cats. Many of the cats were made out of things I'd never even come across before, so I didn't know how to describe them. After I'd examined each cat carefully, I replaced it in its correct position on the shelf.

Then I realized I was tired. I hadn't been able to sleep properly in my Earthmobile, with the wind howling through the air vents and my clothes all soaking wet.

So I climbed straight into Rosie's bed, lay my head upon her comfy pillows, pulled the cat duvet round my shoulders and fell fast asleep.

* * *

This turned out to be my best day on Earth so far. Not only did I enjoy a really nice time at Rosie's; not only did it stop raining; but it was also the day that I discovered fish and chip shops. This is how it happened.

I was driving back along the high street when all the traffic stopped. This often seems to happen, I've noticed, when the red traffic lights are lit. While I was sitting there with nothing much to do, I noticed a shop that was still open. As I've mentioned before, this was quite unusual after it got dark. The shop was called Humphrey Haddock. What a wonderful name for a shop, I thought. As it was open and had such a lovely smell wafting from the doorway, I decided to leave my Earthmobile and have a look.

There was a big queue of people in Humphrey Haddock's. This was not surprising. The smell of food inside was so delicious that I thought I was going to faint.

While I was waiting, I read the menu on the wall.

HADDOCK 'N' CHIPS	PIE, CHIPS 'N' PEAS
HADDOCK 'N' PEAS	SPRING ROLL
HADDOCK, CHIPS 'N' PEAS	ONION BHAJI
COD 'N' CHIPS	CURRY SAUCE
COD 'N' PEAS	FISHCAKE
COD, CHIPS 'N' PEAS	BATTERED SAUSAGE
PIE 'N' CHIPS	MEAT PIE
PIE 'N' PEAS	
CARTON OF MUSHY PEAS WITH GRAVY	

"What would you like, love?" the lady asked me.

"Haddock, Peas 'n' Chips," I said, "for starters. And then..." I wasn't sure. I thought about ordering one of everything, but I didn't want to seem too greedy. "For pudding I'll just have the Battered Sausage, Fishcake and Mushy Peas."

"Right you are."

The lady scooped shovelfuls of chips into a wire basket and spread them out in front of us inside a steamy glass box, then she wrapped each item of my meal inside a little bag. Then she wrapped up the food in a newspaper.

I took out some Earthpennies for the food. "How much is it for the newspaper?" I asked her.

She looked surprised. "The newspaper's free," she explained.

I thought that was very kind. "I'll look forward to reading it," I told her.

"Is this your vehicle?" The policeman was standing by my car.

I didn't say anything. My mouth was full of chips.

"Don't you know this is a one-way street?" he asked me. He was staring (bad manners!) at my three green fingers clasped round my bag of succulent, vinegar-saturated chips.

"I was only driving one way," I told him. "Would you like a chip?"

The policeman glowered at me and took out his notebook and pencil. "Are you offering me a bribe?" he asked suspiciously.

I didn't know what a bribe was. "They didn't have any of those in Humphrey Haddock's," I told him, "but there's a battered sausage if you'd like a taste of that."

The policeman looked a bit startled when I offered him my sausage, but he decided to try a bite. While he was standing there unable to speak, with his mouth crammed full of crispy, hot sausage, I leapt inside my Earthmobile and whizzed away.

All the food from Humphrey Haddock's tasted absolutely wonderful, but the chips tasted nicest of all. Although they only looked like little pieces of wood, they were succulent and crispy. If I could find out the recipe for making chips and take it back home to my planet, I thought, I could make myself a fortune. I decided to save a few of the chips to take round to Rosie's with me. What a nice surprise for her, I thought, if I left her a bag of cold chips. It was the nicest present I could think of.

DEPARTMENT OF INTERPLANETARY STUDIES

TOPIC SHEET 4: THE EARTH

1. Are There Any Ways in Which You Consider Earth People to Be More Advanced Than the Inhabitants of Triangulum?
On Earth they have invented the fish and chip shop. In order to invent this, you first have to find out how to make chips. They have a very special, delicious smell, especially when sprinkled with salt and soaked in lots of vinegar. The mushy peas are good as well. And the crispy haddock.

Fish and chip shops also provide a useful service by giving away free newspapers with every purchase that you make.

There are special shops that sell newspapers on their own without the chips in, but they don't smell as nice.

2. How Friendly Are the Inhabitants of Planet Earth?

The lady who works in the fish and chip shop is very friendly, but the others keep giving me funny looks. They keep staring at my fingers and my antennae.

Chapter Four

The next morning I woke up with an itchy feeling in my nose. "Atishoo!" I went. "Atishoo!"

I couldn't understand why I was sneezing. At home I only sneeze when there's lots of dust about, but there wasn't any dust inside my Earthmobile. It was much too draughty.

I drove to Rosie's house and this time parked right outside her front door. I placed Rosie's chips inside the pocket of my spacesuit, and collected her key from the flowerpot beside the front door. Then I unlocked the door and went inside.

"Atishoo!" I sneezed again. "Atishoo!"

I still didn't know why I was sneezing. I felt sure there wasn't any dust in Rosie's house. "Atishoo!" I went again, as I walked into Rosie's bedroom. "Atishoo!"

On the chest of drawers next to Rosie's bed was a box of coloured tissues. I helped myself to one or two and blew my nose. I'd never had such a runny nose before.

I took out the bag of chips and placed them

in Rosie's drawer. The chips didn't smell as nice when they were cold, but I still thought Rosie would have a lovely surprise when she found them hidden among her hankies and her socks.

Then I sat down on the bed. I was feeling a bit tired. My eyelids felt heavy and my legs were aching, so I pulled off my spaceboots and climbed into bed. I shivered a little as I pulled the cat duvet round my shoulders. It was nice and warm in Rosie's bed...

I slept for quite a long time. My head was aching a bit when I woke up. I climbed out of bed and pulled on my boots and blew my nose again. When I straightened the bed, I noticed some screwed-up tissues underneath the pillow. Perhaps Rosie had the sneezes as well.

Then I looked on the desk. I thought Rosie might have left me a thank you note for helping with her homework, but her Maths book wasn't even opened. Instead, on top of her books was a poster that Rosie had been making. It said:

LOST

A ginger cat with white
tips on her ears

Answers to the name of Gingernut

Last seen on Monday evening

If you have any information about this
lost cat, please

Rosie hadn't finished the poster, but I understood then why she hadn't even checked her homework. She must have been out looking for her cat.

I realized how upset she must have been. Rosie loved cats very much. I even wondered then about all the tissues – perhaps Rosie had been crying.

I decided straight away that I would help her. I would hunt round the house and round the garden. I knew what Gingernut looked like. I felt sure that I could find her before Rosie came home from school.

I started off by searching the house. I know the kind of places where cats are likely to hide because, as I said before, cats are just the same, right across the galaxy. I decided to start at the top of the house and work my way through to the bottom.

I opened the drawers and the cupboards, but I couldn't find the cat. Then I looked under all the beds. "Gingernut!" I shouted. "Come on, Ginger." But Gingernut wasn't there. I rummaged inside the linen baskets and looked through the dirty washing. I opened the door of the airing cupboard and searched among the towels, then I went downstairs.

I peered inside the broom cupboard and sorted through all the dusters. "Gingernut!" I shouted. "Where are you?" The cat was nowhere to be seen. Then I scoured underneath the sink and inside the microwave oven. I searched underneath the ironing board and inside the washing machine, behind the tumble dryer and even inside the cooker.

The cat was nowhere to be found.

Then I went outside to search the garden. I looked underneath the bushes and behind the compost heap. I looked inside the greenhouse and in the branches of the trees. I looked inside the garden shed and...

I didn't find the cat, but I did hear a strange sound. It was a kind of squeak. A very tiny squeak. I looked round. There was nothing there. Just a workbench and a vice, an electric drill and some tool boxes and plant pots and a...

Squeak!

There it was again. It didn't sound like a cat at all, more like a little mouse. It seemed to be coming from an old grey cardigan high up on the shelf. I climbed on to the workbench to investigate. I stood up on tiptoe and peeped inside the cardigan and... I could hardly believe my eyes. There was a cluster of tiny, weeny ginger balls of fur with Gingernut sitting proudly in the middle, licking and washing them. So that's what had happened to her! She'd crept away and found a nest where she could have her kittens. I just stood and stared at the little balls of scraggy fur. They had tiny closed eyes and flattened ears. I thought they looked absolutely wonderful.

Then I realized that Gingernut must be hungry. There wasn't any cat food in the shed. If nobody knew where she was, she wouldn't have been fed for at least two days. I decided to go and fetch her some food and a saucer of milk from the house.

It wasn't hard to find the cat food. I saw the Tiddles labels straight away inside the glass-fronted cupboard. I could tell what was inside them from the pictures of cats, their whiskers buried in various food bowls, munching away contentedly. The problem was that the cat food was in tin boxes and when I took one down I couldn't find how to open it.

I stared at the label of *Tiddles Pilchards in Tomato Sauce* with its picture of a cat just like Gingernut gobbling down her fish, but I didn't know how to lift the lid. The top wasn't even loose. I turned the tin box over in my hand, searching for instructions. There were no instructions at all.

I was flummoxed.

I shook it, but nothing happened. I tried to squash it in my hand, but I only hurt my fingers. I tore off the label, but underneath was only a shiny, metal surface. There seemed to be no way of opening it at all.

Atishoo! I sneezed, as I thought about what to do. *Atishoo, aaatishoo!*

I don't normally give in easily. I'm quite good at solving problems. I opened a drawer beside the sink and found some knives and forks. I took out the longest, sharpest knife that I could find and tried to cut the metal, but the big, sharp knife hardly left a mark.

Then I tried stabbing it with a great big fork, but the prongs wouldn't even go through.

"Don't give up, Haddock," I told myself. "I'm sure you can do it. Aaatishoo!" Then I remembered the workbench in the shed, with its rows of tools and electric drill. I picked up the tin box, a milk bottle and a saucer and carried them outside.

I tried opening the cat food with some of the tools that were hanging from the workbench. I made several holes, but still the lid wouldn't come off. Then I found an electric drill and drilled holes in the lid, but I still couldn't get the food out. When Gingernut smelled the fish, she jumped down from her nest and started weaving in and out of my legs. "Just hang on a minute, Gingernut," I explained. "We're nearly there now."

The next thing I found was an electric saw. I fastened it to the end of the drill. That was much better. Before long I was sawing the tin thing in half. The cat food made the blade all sticky and the saw made a high-pitched, whining sound that I thought might have frightened the kittens, but they didn't seem to mind.

The electric saw was so loud that I didn't hear the car arrive. So there I was, standing in the garden shed, with two halves of a tin thing of Tiddles, one in each hand, when I heard voices in the yard. "Burglars! We've had burglars!" I heard the little boy shout.

Oh, dear, I thought. I didn't notice any burglars. I haven't seen anybody prowling about. Then all of a sudden my triangle started to tingle...

I'd left the back door wide open when I'd dashed out with the cat food. The front door was unlocked and the key was lying somewhere in the kitchen. When the family went upstairs they would have seen their linen basket tipped over and their dirty washing scattered on the floor. When they went inside their bedrooms they would have seen the drawers half open. That was how

I'd left things when I'd been searching for Gingernut. I was intending to go back afterwards and tidy everything away, but I hadn't had time to do it yet.

I gave Gingernut her cat food, poured some milk into her saucer and then I wondered what to do. What if they really thought I was a burglar? What if they thought I'd gone there to steal things from the house?

Just then I heard a siren wailing. It seemed to be coming up the street, getting louder and louder. I glanced down at Gingernut lapping up her milk. No thanks, of course, for all my efforts. No appreciation. And no help either from a cat in a time of trouble like this.

The siren wailed louder than ever. In fact it seemed to be coming up the drive. Both my sets of three green fingers trembled slightly as I stood the two halves of cat food back upon the bench. A siren meant a police car and a police car seemed to mean trouble. I didn't know what to do. I didn't see how I could escape. My Earthmobile was parked in the driveway, right in front of the house.

"We've left everything just as we found it," I heard the man explaining as the police cars pulled up in the yard. "We haven't touched anything in case you want to take some fingerprints."

I looked down at the two halves of shiny metal. My fingerprints would be all over them, but there was no point in wiping them off. My Triangulumprints would be unmistakable. And they would also be on the washing machine and the microwave and the door handles and the handle of the knife... all over the house in fact.

"There's a big knife in the middle of the kitchen table!" I heard the little boy shout. "The burglar was going to stab us!"

I started feeling sick. I didn't know what to do. I was only trying to be helpful.

"And he's hidden some horrible cold chips in my sock drawer. Ugh!"

My stomach started sinking. Everything

I'd done was wrong.

"We'd better search the premises."

I didn't know what premises were, but I had a feeling that it might include the shed. I began to crawl underneath the workbench. What would happen if they found me? My spaceship would be coming to collect me in a few weeks' time. I didn't think the pilot would wait until I got out of prison.

I curled up underneath the workbench with my arms wrapped round my knees. I hoped they wouldn't see my silver spacesuit glistening in the darkness.

The shed door creaked open. "We'll have a look in here," the policeman shouted. "I don't think they'll be far away somehow."

From my position underneath the bench, I could see the policeman's big black shoes walking nearer and nearer. As he edged towards the bench, I could see his long black laces trailing down. Beside him was a policewoman. I could see her black tights and low-heeled black shoes as she started searching the shed. They were both standing very close to the bench. I felt sure they were going to find me. Whatever could I do?

I heard the policeman picking up the saw. "There's been something fishy going on in here," he said.

"Very fishy. It looks like blood to me," the policewoman said. "Or do you think it might be human flesh?"

I tried not to sigh. Even I can recognize pilchards in tomato sauce and I'm from a different planet. I didn't think she'd make a very good detective.

They looked round the shed, but they didn't look underneath the workbench. I thought I was going to escape. I thought I might be all right. I thought they might not notice me. That is, until my nose started itching. I felt a big sneeze coming on.

I tried to hold my breath. I tried to hold my nose. I tried to squash my nostrils together. I screwed up my body in a great big knot to try and stop the sneeze escaping.

Just one second while the police walked back towards the door and I thought I might possibly survive and then...

A-a-a-a-a-a-tishoooooo!

It was the biggest sneeze in all the world, the biggest sneeze you've ever heard. The biggest sneeze in the galaxy.

"What was that?"

There was a second's pause, but that was all. I didn't wait for the policeman to search underneath the bench. I didn't wait for the policewoman to compare my fingerprints with those on the box of Tiddles. I just sprang up and hurtled like a meteor out of the shed door. The policewoman turned to chase me but Gingernut was in the way. She tripped over the cat and collided with the policeman. That gave me just enough time to get away.

I tore out of the shed and straight across the yard. I leapt into my Earthmobile. I pressed the starter motor and fired on all three jets. I turned on the high-speed turbines and whirred my triangular tail fins into action. I activated the emergency speed programme and twizzled round the steering triangle. Of course, turning the vehicle wasn't easy because there were two police cars standing in the drive.

"Stop that vehicle!" the policeman shouted, stumbling out of the shed.

"Arrest that burglar!" the policewoman shouted, waving her arms in the air.

But my jets were firing and my turbines charging. I slalomed round the police cars standing in the drive. I skidded round the corner to the gate. I looked behind me and saw the policeman running to his car. But he was too late. I was already whizzing out of the gate and down the road towards the high street. I could hear the police siren wailing, but I was on my way.

Down past the squashed zebra and the place where the pelican sits. Down past Humphrey Haddock's chip shop, out on the open road. In my side fin mirrors I could see the blue flashing light of the police car. It started catching up with me when the traffic lights turned red and all the cars slowed down. The blue light got much nearer when I had to stop for a crowd of schoolchildren straggling across the road, but soon I was zooming off again. Jets firing, tail fins gleaming, triangle tingling with the full force of my high-speed autocharge. I took one last look at the blue flashing light in my side fin mirrors, but now it was a long, long way behind me. A long way in the distance.

I sped out into the countryside and then I found a little lane. It wasn't big enough for a police car, but just right for my Earthmobile. The bushes were scratching at my paintwork but that didn't matter. All that mattered was that I'd found the perfect hiding place. I parked behind a big tree and watched the blue light of the police car as it sped up and down the road searching for the silver-suited burglar.

* * *

When the police car had gone, I climbed out of my Earthmobile and decided to explore. I daren't go back to the town again just yet.

I kept an eye open for police cars and went for a wander down the lane while I thought about what to do. After a minute or two I arrived at a small field. In the middle of the field was the smallest house I'd ever seen. It was a bit like a shed but rounded at the ends. It had wheels underneath but it didn't seem to have an engine. Poking out of the roof was a crooked, metal chimney.

Fastened to one of the windows was a notice:

CARAVAN TO RENT

Ask at the farmhouse for details

Chapter Five

So, now I'm living inside my caravan and my assignment on Earth is almost over.

The caravan is wonderful. It has gaslights on the walls that burn with a little flame when I light them with a match. It has a tiny fridge, just like Rosie's, where I keep all my cartons of milk shake. It has an old-fashioned stove that burns logs and pieces of coal. I can sit next to it and warm my hands and I can stand a pan of milk on top to warm up for my drinking chocolate. At the side is a little oven where I can heat up my fish 'n' chips from Humphrey Haddock's.

At the bottom of the caravan is a very small bed built into the wall. That's where I sleep, underneath a pile of blankets and a nice soft eiderdown.

As soon as I saw the caravan, I knew it would make a perfect place for me to stay. Just the right size. And it doesn't cost much in rent, so I have plenty of Earthpennies left for my food and anything else I need. I've been making a few improvements as well, just to brighten things up. The field outside is filled with beautiful yellow flowers. They're called dandelions. I pick them and make displays like the ones in Rosie's house, except that mine are in empty milk shake cartons all round the room. I've crayoned a notice like Rosie's as well, to go on the front door. A notice with my name on. It says:

Haddock's Caravan

When the nice lady at Humphrey Haddock's gives me a newspaper with my chips, I cut out the pictures and stick them on the wall. Some of them are a bit greasy but they do smell nice.

The most important event occurred after I'd been living here for the first few days. When I came home, there was something different about the place. I wasn't sure what it was – a different smell in the air perhaps. Before I got into bed that night, I noticed a slight hollow on the eiderdown, just as if a very small person had been sitting there. I couldn't understand it. I wondered if there might be another homeless alien who wanted to share my caravan with me.

The next night the mystery was solved. When I came home, there wasn't just a little dip in the middle of the bed. There was a furry creature lying there as if it owned the place. It was fast asleep and had its tail curled right round its whiskers. Yes, you might have guessed – a cat. A stray cat who'd been searching for a new owner and a home. And here I am. And here she is. She's a black cat with long hair and gingery patches round her ears, and she loves to eat fish 'n' chips.

I've tried to find the recipe for chips. I've looked through dozens of cookery books in the library and in the bookshop in th
street, but not one of them explaine
magical ingredients. I think the rec

making chips must be a very closely-guarded secret on planet Earth. Fortunately my money has lasted well, and I've been able to afford all the chips I need from Humphrey Haddock's.

So, here I am, finishing off my assignment, and it won't be long now before the spaceship arrives to take me back home to Triangulum.

When I first arrived here, I was expecting someone to welcome me. When there was no one to greet me or even take notice of me, I started feeling very lonely. I was hoping to find a family to take me in and make me feel at home.

That's why when I first found Rosie's house I so much wanted to live there. I thought I would never feel homesick, sharing Rosie's room and playing with her cats and snuggling down underneath her duvet.

What I've learned now, of course, is the most important thing in my assignment. I've learned how to make myself welcome on planet Earth and I've learned how to make my own home. It may not be a great big house with a long driveway and roses round the door, but it's comfy and snug and warm and it's all mine. What I've learned to do is look after myself, all alone in a strange, inhospitable planet. I'm very very proud of how much I've managed to achieve.

I've made friends now as well. I've made friends with the people at Humphrey Haddock's chip shop and at the library where I've been looking through the books. I've made friends with the schoolchildren who've admired my Earthmobile and asked me to give them rides.

And, of course, I've found a very special friend as well. Not the sort of friend I was expecting. I assumed another little girl would want to be my friend, but that was not to be.

My new friend welcomes me each time I come home, weaving in and out of my legs to see if I've brought her any food. She sits down and eats her meals with me and licks all the paper bags afterwards. When I sit by the wood-burning stove, she climbs on my knee and purrs and holds up her head so that I can stroke her and tickle her ears. I suppose you can guess what I've called her. I've called her after my favourite thing on planet Earth. I've had to alter the notice that I'd made to stick on the front door. No longer does it say

Haddock's Caravan

It now says:

Haddock 'n' Chips

The Department
of Interplanetary Studies
(Triangulum Division)

---

is delighted to confer the

Star Prize for Intergalactic Assignments

to

Haddock

For Her Outstanding Study of
Life on Planet Earth Entitled:

Haddock 'n' Chips

This is to certify that Haddock
has been awarded the
Intergalactic Order of Merit:

The Golden Triangle

TITCH JOHNSON

Mark Haddon

Titch Johnson wants to be special. He's tired of being average and normal and ordinary; he wants to be the best at something. But he's not a champion runner like Monster Dixon and he doesn't have great ideas like Jarvis – the only thing he's any good at is balancing a fork on the end of his nose! As it turns out, though, this skill is not nearly as useless as it seems.